Geronimo Stilton
ENGLISH!

28 HIGH-TECH 日新月異的科技

新雅文化事業有限公司
www.sunya.com.hk

Geronimo Stilton English
HIGH-TECH　日新月異的科技

作　　者：Geronimo Stilton 謝利連摩·史提頓
譯　　者：申倩
責任編輯：王燕參
封面繪圖：Giuseppe Facciotto
插圖繪畫：Claudio Cernuschi, Andrea Denegri, Daria Cerchi
內文設計：Angela Ficarelli, Raffaella Picozzi
出　　版：新雅文化事業有限公司
　　　　　香港英皇道499號北角工業大廈18樓
　　　　　電話：（852）2138 7998
　　　　　傳真：（852）2597 4003
　　　　　網址：http://www.sunya.com.hk
　　　　　電郵：marketing@sunya.com.hk
發　　行：香港聯合書刊物流有限公司
　　　　　香港新界大埔汀麗路36號中華商務印刷大廈3字樓
　　　　　電話：（852）2150 2100　　傳真：（852）2407 3062
　　　　　電郵：info@suplogistics.com.hk
印　　刷：C & C Offset Printing Co.,Ltd
　　　　　香港新界大埔汀麗路36號
版　　次：二〇一二年七月初版
　　　　　10 9 8 7 6 5 4 3 2 1

ISBN: 978-962-08-5624-2
© 2008 Edizioni Piemme S.p.A., Via Tiziano 32 - 20145 Milano - Italia
International Rights © 2008 Atlantyca S.p.A. - via Leopardi, 8, Milano - Italy
© 2012 for this Work in Traditional Chinese language, Sun Ya Publications (HK) Ltd.
18/F, North Point Industrial Building, 499 King's Road, Hong Kong.
Published and printed in Hong Kong

CONTENTS
目錄

BENJAMIN'S CLASSMATES

班哲文的老師和同學們

Maestra Topitilla
托比蒂拉·德·托比莉斯

Rarin
拉琳

Diego
迪哥

Rupa
露芭

Tui
杜爾

David
大衛

Sakura
櫻花

Mohamed
穆哈麥德

Tian Kai
田凱

Oliver
奧利佛

Milenko
米蘭哥

Trippo
特里普

Carmen
卡敏

Atina
阿提娜

Esmeralda
愛絲梅拉達

Pandora
潘朵拉

Takeshi
北野

Kuti
菊花

Benjamin
班哲文

Hsing
阿星

Laura
羅拉

Kiku
奇哥

Antonia
安東妮婭

Liza
麗莎

GERONIMO AND HIS FRIENDS
謝利連摩和他的家鼠朋友們

謝利連摩・史提頓 Geronimo Stilton
一個古怪的傢伙，簡直可以說是一隻笨拙的文化鼠。他是《鼠民公報》的總裁，正花盡心思改變報紙業的歷史。

菲・史提頓 Tea Stilton
謝利連摩的妹妹，她是《鼠民公報》的特派記者，同時也是一個運動愛好者。

班哲文・史提頓 Benjamin Stilton
謝利連摩的小侄兒，常被叔叔稱作「我的小乳酪」，是一隻感情豐富的小老鼠。

潘朵拉・華之鼠 Pandora Woz
柏蒂・活力鼠的姨甥女、班哲文最好的朋友，是一隻活潑開朗的小老鼠。

柏蒂・活力鼠 Patty Spring
美麗迷人的電視新聞工作者，致力於她熱愛的電視事業。

賴皮 Trappola
謝利連摩的表弟，非常喜歡食物，風趣幽默，是一隻饞嘴、愛開玩笑的老鼠，善於將歡樂傳遞給每一隻鼠。

麗萍姑媽 Zia Lippa
謝利連摩的姑媽，對鼠十分友善，又和藹可親，只想將最好的給身邊的鼠。

艾拿 Iena
謝利連摩的好朋友，充滿活力，熱愛各項運動，他希望能把對運動的熱誠傳給謝利連摩。

史奎克・愛管閒事鼠 Ficcanaso Squitt
謝利連摩的好朋友，是一個非常有頭腦的私家偵探，總是穿着一件黃色的乾濕褸。

WHAT ARE YOU DOING?
你在做什麼？

親愛的小朋友，今天班哲文和潘朵拉放學後到我辦公室來找我。你知道他們找我有什麼事嗎？看在一千塊莫澤雷勒乳酪的份上，他們希望我給他們上一節電腦課！但我必須坦白地告訴你一個小秘密：我對高科技不太在行，實際上我是一個科技盲！還好今天我妹妹菲也在辦公室，她可是這方面的專家，可以給我們講解有關的知識。你也跟我們一起學習有關電腦的詞彙吧……當然是英語詞彙啦！

download photographs
下載照片
proofread a book
校對書籍
write an e-mail
寫電子郵件

I'm proofreading a book.

跟我謝利連摩‧史提頓一起學英文，
就像玩遊戲一樣簡單好玩！

你可以一邊看着圖畫一邊讀。
以下有幾個標誌，你要特別留意：

當看到 標誌時，你可以聽CD，
一邊聽，一邊跟着朗讀，還可以跟
着一起唱歌。

當看到 ★ 標誌時，你可以和朋友
們一起玩遊戲，或者嘗試回答問
題。題目很簡單，它們對鞏固你所
學過的內容很有幫助。

當看到 標誌時，你要注意看一
下格子裏的生字，反覆唸幾遍，掌
握發音。

最後，不要忘記完成小測驗和練習
冊裏的問題！看看你有多聰明吧。

祝大家學得開開心心！

謝利連摩‧史提頓

USING A COMPUTER
使用電腦

　　菲帶我們去了編輯室，並向我們講解怎樣使用電腦。不過，在學習用電腦之前，班哲文和潘朵拉要先學習一下電腦各部分的名稱用英語怎麼說，例如鍵盤、印表機、手提電腦……很多很多新詞彙啊！你也跟着他們一起學習吧。

computer	laptop	desktop	screen	file

folder	CD or DVD player	keyboard	mouse	telephone

scanner	printer	webcam	digital camera	speakers

turn on the computer
開啟電腦

turn off the computer
關掉電腦

screen

desktop

keyboard

Have you ever used a computer, kids?

Yes, we have. Lots of times.

Have you ever drawn a picture on the computer?

No, never.

Neither have I!

Have you ever written an e-mail?

No, I haven't.

Neither have I!

Would you like to learn how to?

Oh, yes!

A SONG FOR YOU!

Track 1

My Computer

Have you ever used a computer?
Have you ever written an e-mail?
Computers are fantastic,
you can use them to
learn many things.

Come on, kids, it's easy!
Would you like to
write an e-mail?
Oh, yes, yes we would.
Can we do it now?
Computers are fantastic,
you can use them to
learn many things.

Have you ever used a computer?
你們有沒有用過電腦？

Yes, we have. 有，我們用過。

No, we haven't. 沒有，我們沒用過。

E-MAIL 電子郵件

　　電子郵箱讓我們可以很快地把郵件發送到世界各地，非常方便。潘朵拉想給她住在法國的朋友寫一封電子郵件，但她不知道該怎樣做，於是菲教她如何操作。你也跟着一起學習吧！

e-mail address　電郵地址	click　點擊
address book　地址簿	edit　編輯
subject　主題	cut　剪下
attachment　附件	copy　複製
message　信息	paste　貼上
open　開啟舊檔	save　儲存檔案
close　關閉	print　列印
place the cursor over　把鼠標移到	

I would like to write a message to my friends who live in France.

Yes, anywhere with an Internet connection!

Can we send a message anywhere in the world?

anywhere
任何地方

 10

★ 試着用英語説出：「我想寫封信給我的朋友們。」

菲還告訴我們，寫電子郵件時可以利用不同的表情符號表達自己的情緒，它們是用英文字母和標點符號組成的，看看下面其中一些例子吧，很有趣的。

:) I am happy! 我很開心！

:D I am very happy! 我非常開心！

:O What a surprise! 真驚訝！

:(I'm sad! 我很傷心！

:'(I'm very sad! 我非常傷心！

:-# I can't say anymore! 我不能再說下去了！

:\ I'm angry! 我很生氣！

:@ I'm very angry! 我非常生氣！

:$ I'm shy! 我很害羞！

:S I'm puzzled! 我很疑惑！

+O) I'm sick! 我生病了！

;) I'm joking. / I'm winking. 我在開玩笑。／我在眨眼睛。

11

PEN FRIENDS 筆友

　　菲打開電子郵箱，她剛剛收到一封來自美國筆友的郵件，這位朋友叫做占姆，是一位攝影師！於是菲提議班哲文和潘朵拉也給占姆寫封信介紹他們自己，這可是建立友誼的好機會呀！

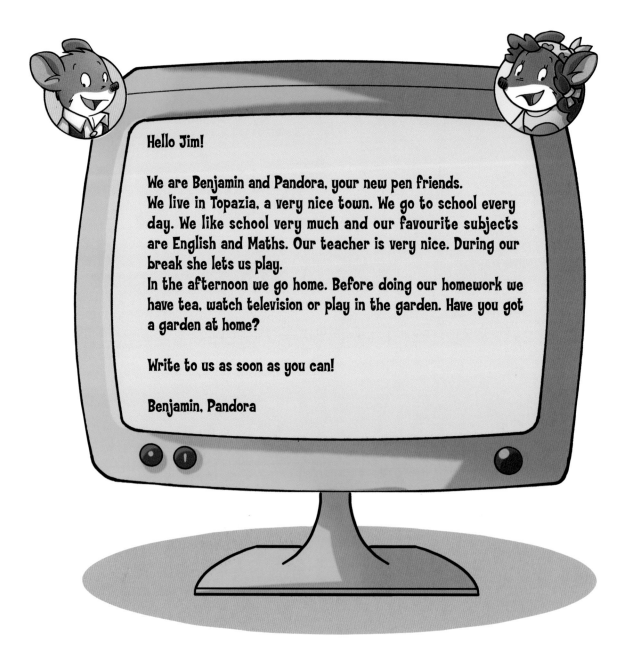

Hello Jim!

We are Benjamin and Pandora, your new pen friends.
We live in Topazia, a very nice town. We go to school every day. We like school very much and our favourite subjects are English and Maths. Our teacher is very nice. During our break she lets us play.
In the afternoon we go home. Before doing our homework we have tea, watch television or play in the garden. Have you got a garden at home?

Write to us as soon as you can!

Benjamin, Pandora

★ 試着讀出班哲文和潘朵拉寫給占姆的信吧。

班哲文和潘朵拉發出了郵件後，不一會兒就收到了占姆的回覆。電子郵件真是太方便快捷了！下面就是占姆寫的回信，請與班哲文和潘朵拉一起讀出來吧。

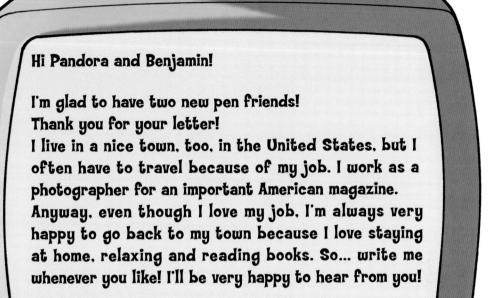

Hi Pandora and Benjamin!

I'm glad to have two new pen friends!
Thank you for your letter!
I live in a nice town, too, in the United States, but I often have to travel because of my job. I work as a photographer for an important American magazine. Anyway, even though I love my job, I'm always very happy to go back to my town because I love staying at home, relaxing and reading books. So... write me whenever you like! I'll be very happy to hear from you!

Love, Jim

在看完占姆的回信後，菲告訴班哲文和潘朵拉，英式英語和美式英語其實是有少許區別的，下面是其中一些例子，你也一起來學習吧。

BRITISH ENGLISH 英式英語	AMERICAN ENGLISH 美式英語	CHINESE 中文
lift	elevator	升降機
autumn	fall	秋天
football	soccer	足球
sweets	candy	糖果
garden	yard	園子
break	recess	小息
pavement	sidewalk	行人道
underground	subway	行人隧道
postman	mailman	郵差
skipping rope	jumping rope	跳繩
trainers	sneakers	運動鞋
wellies	boots	靴子

THE INTERNET 互聯網

接着，菲給班哲文和潘朵拉講解一些關於使用互聯網的詞彙，你也一起來學習吧。

Internet service provider 互聯網服務供應商
account 帳户
username 使用者名稱
password 密碼
server 伺服器
website 網站
webpage 網頁
home page 首頁
on-line 在線
hardware 硬件
software 軟件

What's the Internet?

The Internet is a network that connects computers all over the world.

Is the Internet useful?

Yes, because you can find lots of information very quickly.

班哲文和潘朵拉聽完菲的講解後，已急不及待想使用互聯網瀏覽網頁，不過我提醒他們一件事，就是使用互聯網時最好有成年人陪同啊！

Explore the Internet, but only if there is an adult with you!

connect to the Internet
連接到互聯網
surf the web
瀏覽網頁
search
搜尋

Yes, I do. I often search for information before writing my articles!

Yes, sure! Let's do it together though!

Can I connect to the Internet, Uncle G?

Do you often surf the web, Aunt Tea?

★ 試着用英語說出：「世界各地」。

TELEVISION, MP3 PLAYER, MOBILE PHONE
電視機、音樂播放器、手提電話

今天《鼠民公報》的專欄會為大家介紹不同的科技產品，例如電視機、音樂播放器、手提電話等，一起來看看吧。

There are so many things that make our life more pleasant and comfortable: television, radio, MP3 player, mobile phone!

You're right! When I go jogging, I listen to music with my MP3 player. It's fantastic!

Mobile phones are very useful: you can make or receive calls anywhere.

You always have to be careful to be polite though. For example it's best to switch it off when you are having a meal with your friends or your family, so you don't disturb other people.

我真是一個科技盲，連用手提電話發短訊也不會呢，於是史丹塔便教我如何利用手提電話發短訊。

Living with Technology

A mobile phone is ringing,
I rush to turn the TV off
and turn down the radio
which was playing loud rock music!

I prepare my MP3 player
to go jogging in the park,
listening to my favourite music
with my little dog Bob!

LET'S PLAY! 一起來玩吧！

　　班哲文和潘朵拉今天真是獲益良多，但他們的驚喜還沒完呢：這時他們的朋友特里普、櫻花和迪哥也來了！於是我提議大家來玩一個遊戲，這個遊戲能考考大家對高科技產品的掌握。想知道自己有多厲害，你也一起來玩玩吧。

	A	B	C	D
1	電子郵件	桌面	鍵盤	光碟機
2	滑鼠	資料夾	電腦	網絡攝影機
3	印表機	手提電腦	掃描器	數碼相機
4	屏幕	電話	喇叭	電視機

HOW TO PLAY

❶ Each player takes turns taking a card and reading the matches written on it. Then, looking at the grid, he says the name of the corresponding object... in English, of course!

❷ The player who makes the fewest mistakes wins.

C4
A1
D2
C2

A2
B3
D1
B2

C3
A4
D3
B1

D4
C1
A3
B4

⭐ 你也可以和家人或朋友一起玩以下遊戲：兩人一組，一個說出物品的位置，另一個則說出對應物品的名稱，當然是用英語說啦！例如：

D2　　　webcam

19

〈紀錄片需要找作家〉

謝利連摩：救命啊！有鯊魚！而且⋯⋯牠們很巨型！

班哲文：不用擔心，叔叔，牠們是鯊魚，但是牠們是⋯⋯

班哲文：……在屏幕上！

謝利連摩：你說得對，班哲文，但這些高清電視機的畫面真是逼真得令人難以置信。

柏蒂：我們再試一次吧？

謝利連摩：好的，我現在可以啦！

達科他：正如我所說的……我們想出版一本書來配合這套紀錄片。

柏蒂：賣書所得的款項將用作慈善用途。

達科他：但我們需要一位著名的作家來寫這本書……就像你，謝利連摩！

謝利連摩：好的，我們繼續看下一段影片吧，我會把重點記下來。

柏蒂：我們來看看關於螃蟹入侵的那段吧！

達科他：好呀，那段很有趣！

柏蒂：我們在一個很遙遠的小島上。
一天早上，我們醒來時……
達科他：……整個地面變成紅色一片，
而且很硬。

原來整個地面都被螃蟹覆蓋了。

達科他：然後突然之間……　　　　　　柏蒂：……什麼東西跳了出來……

柏蒂：……是一隻巨大的螃蟹！
謝利連摩：啊啊啊！
班哲文：叔叔，牠仍然只是在電視機上！

謝利連摩：好的，好的，繼續看吧。
達科他：看黑海盜那段？
柏蒂：好的，那太完美了。

達科他：我們一起來看影片吧！
謝利連摩：嗯……不，不用那麼麻煩了，只需把故事告訴我就可以了！

半小時之後……
達科他：……跟著我們便說再見……
柏蒂：……跟那個著名的黑海盜！
謝利連摩：好了！我下星期便會交第一章，但有一個條件……

謝利連摩：我不想再看那DVD了。
達科他：哈！哈！哈！好的！

TEST 小測驗

⭐ 1. 用英語説出下面的句子。

(a) 你在做什麼？ What ... ... ?

(b) 我正在寫電子郵件。 I'm ... ...

(c) 我正在下載照片到我的手提電腦裏。 I'm ... ... onto my ... !

⭐ 2. 「你有沒有用過電腦？」這句話用英語該怎麼説？圈出相應的英文句子。

Have you ever used a computer?

Have you ever written an e-mail?

⭐ 3. 用英語説出以下詞彙。

(a) 手提電腦

(b) 電話

(c) 印表機

(d) 數碼相機

⭐ 4. 讀出下面的句子，並用中文説出句子的意思。

(a) Do you often surf the web?

(b) Yes, I do. I often search for information before writing my articles!

DICTIONARY 詞典

（英、粵、普發聲）

A

account　帳戶

address book　地址簿

adult　成年人

angry　生氣

anywhere　任何地方

attachment　附件

autumn　秋天

B

boots　靴子

break　小息 (普：課間休息)

C

candy　糖果

CD or DVD player
　光碟機

charity　慈善

click　點擊

close　關閉

comfortable　舒適的

computer　電腦

condition　條件

connection　連接

copy　複製

crab　螃蟹

cursor　鼠標

cut　剪下

D

desktop　桌面

digital camera　數碼相機

disturb　騷擾

download　下載

E

edit　編輯

elevator　升降機

e-mail　電子郵件

e-mail address　電郵地址

F

fall　秋天

file　檔案

folder　資料夾

football　足球

G

garden　園子

H

hardware　硬件

home page　首頁

homework　功課

I

important　重要的

information　資料

Internet　互聯網

invasion　入侵

J

jogging　緩步跑

jumping rope　跳繩

K

keyboard　鍵盤

L

laptop　手提電腦

lift　升降機

M

magazine　雜誌

mailman　郵差

message　信息

mobile phone　手提電話

mouse　滑鼠

music　音樂

N

network　網絡

O

on-line　在線

open　開啟舊檔

P

password　密碼

paste　貼上

pavement　行人道

pen friends　筆友

photographer　攝影師

photographs　相片

picture　圖畫

pirate　海盜

polite　有禮貌

postman　郵差

print　列印

printer　印表機

proofread　校對

provider　供應商

publish　出版

puzzled　疑惑

R

radio　收音機

receive　收到

recess　小息（普：課間休息）

S

save　儲存檔案

scanner　掃描器

screen　屏幕

search　搜尋

send　寄

server　伺服器（普：服務器）

shark　鯊魚

shy　害羞

sidewalk　行人道

skipping rope　跳繩

sneakers　運動鞋

soccer 足球

software 軟件

speakers 喇叭

subject 主題

subway 行人隧道

surprise 驚訝

sweets 糖果

T

teacher 老師

telephone 電話

television 電視機

trainers 運動鞋

turn off 關掉

turn on 開啟

U

underground 行人隧道

username 使用者名稱

V

video 影片

W

webcam 網絡攝影機

webpage 網頁

website 網站

wellies 靴子

Y

yard 園子

看在一千塊莫澤雷勒乳酪的份上，你學得開心嗎？很開心，對不對？好極了！跟你一起跳舞唱歌我也很開心！我等着你下次繼續跟班哲文和潘朵拉一起玩一起學英語呀。現在要說再見了，當然是用英語說啦！

GERONIMO'S ISLAND
老鼠島地圖

1. 大冰湖
2. 毛結冰山
3. 滑溜溜冰川
4. 鼠皮疙瘩山
5. 鼠基斯坦
6. 鼠坦尼亞
7. 吸血鬼山
8. 鐵板鼠火山
9. 硫磺湖
10. 貓止步關
11. 醉酒峯
12. 黑森林
13. 吸血鬼谷
14. 發冷山
15. 黑影關
16. 客嗇鼠城堡
17. 自然保護公園
18. 拉斯鼠維加斯海岸
19. 化石森林
20. 小鼠湖
21. 中鼠湖
22. 大鼠湖
23. 諾比奧拉乳酪峯
24. 肯尼貓城堡
25. 巨杉山谷
26. 梵提娜乳酪泉
27. 硫磺沼澤
28. 間歇泉
29. 田鼠谷
30. 瘋鼠谷
31. 蚊子沼澤
32. 史卓奇諾乳酪城堡
33. 鼠哈拉沙漠
34. 喘氣駱駝綠洲
35. 第一山
36. 熱帶叢林
37. 蚊子谷

Geronimo Stilton

EXERCISE BOOK
練習冊

想知道自己對 HIGH-TECH 掌握了多少，
趕快打開後面的練習完成它吧！

ENGLISH!

28 HIGH-TECH 日新月異的科技

WHAT ARE YOU DOING?
你在做什麼？

★ 他們在說什麼？根據圖畫，選出適當的詞彙填在橫線上，完成他們的對話。

downloading	laptop	doing
writing	proofreading	

1. What are you _____, Aunt Tea?

2. I'm _____ photographs onto my _____ !

3. I'm _____ a book.

4. I'm _____ an e-mail.

USING A COMPUTER
使用電腦

⭐ 班哲文學會了很多關於科技產品的英文詞彙。他想考考你，看看你學會了多少。根據圖畫，從下面選出適當的詞彙填在橫線上。

laptop	keyboard	webcam
screen	folder	telephone
printer	digital camera	speakers

1.

_____

2.

_____

3.

_____

4.

_____

5.

_____

6.

_____

7.

_____

8.

_____

9.

_____

E-MAIL 電子郵件

⭐ 你知道下面這些與寫電子郵件有關的英文詞彙的意思嗎？把它們與相配的中文詞彙用線連起來。

1. e-mail address •   • A. 儲存檔案

2. paste •   • B. 點擊

3. address book •   • C. 編輯

4. subject •   • D. 電郵地址

5. attachment •   • E. 複製

6. edit •   • F. 貼上

7. cut •   • G. 主題

8. copy •   • H. 地址簿

9. save •   • I. 附件

10. click •   • J. 剪下

EMOTICONS 表情符號

★ 下面的表情符號各代表什麼意思？選出適當的句子，把代表答案的英文字母填在空格內。

A. I'm happy!　　　　　E. I'm sad!

B. I'm angry!　　　　　F. I'm joking.

C. I'm shy!　　　　　　G. What a surprise!

D. I can't say anymore!　H. I'm puzzled!

1. :) 　☐

2. :) 　☐

3. :(　☐

4. :O 　☐

5. :\ 　☐

6. :-# 　☐

7. :$ 　☐

8. :s 　☐

BRITISH AND AMERICAN ENGLISH 英式和美式英語

★ 把下面意思相同的詞彙用線連起來。

BRITISH ENGLISH	AMERICAN ENGLISH
1. postman	mailman
2. break	fall
3. football	elevator
4. autumn	recess
5. underground	soccer
6. pavement	subway
7. trainers	sidewalk
8. lift	sneakers

THE INTERNET 互聯網

⭐ 班哲文他們在討論關於使用互聯網的事。根據圖畫，從下面選出適當的詞彙填在橫線上，完成他們的對話。

information	connect	surf
search	together	

1. 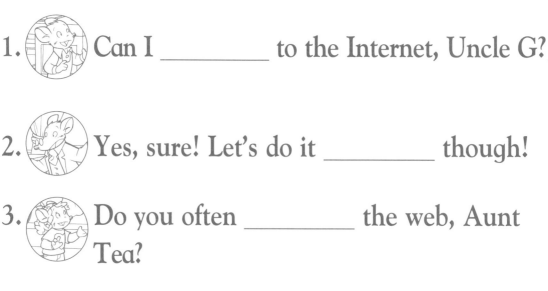 Can I _____ to the Internet, Uncle G?

2. Yes, sure! Let's do it _____ though!

3. Do you often _____ the web, Aunt Tea?

4. Yes, I do. I often _____ for _____ before writing my articles!

.6.

TELEVISION, MP3 PLAYER, MOBILE PHONE 電視機、音樂播放器、手提電話

⭐ 讀出下面的句子，它們分別對應下面哪一幅圖畫？把代表答案的英文字母填在空格內。

A. When I go jogging, I listen to music with my MP3 player.

B. Television and radio make our life more pleasant and comfortable.

C. Mobile phones are very useful: you can make or receive calls anywhere.

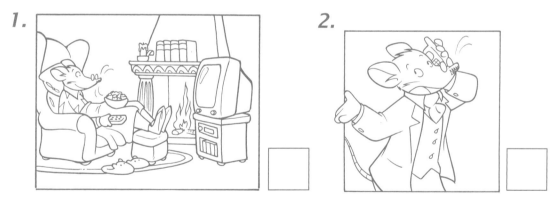

1.

2.

3.

ANSWERS 答案

TEST 小測驗

1. (a) What <u>are</u> <u>you</u> <u>doing</u>?

   (b) I'm <u>writing</u> <u>an</u> <u>e-mail</u>.

   (c) I'm <u>downloading</u> <u>photographs</u> onto my <u>laptop</u>!

2. Have you ever used a computer?

3. (a) laptop   (b) telephone   (c) printer   (d) digital camera

4. (a) 你是否常常瀏覽網頁？

   (b) 是的，我在寫文章前常常會上網搜尋資料。

EXERCISE BOOK 練習冊

P.1

1. doing   2. downloading, laptop   3. proofreading   4. writing

P.2

1. printer   2. laptop   3. screen   4. speakers   5. telephone   6. webcam

7. keyboard   8. folder   9. digital camera

P.3

1. D   2. F   3. H   4. G   5. I   6. C

7. J   8. E   9. A   10. B

P.4

1. F   2. A   3. E   4. G   5. B   6. D   7. C   8. H

P.5

1. postman, mailman   2. break, recess   3. football, soccer   4. autumn, fall

5. underground, subway   6. pavement, sidewalk   7. trainers, sneakers   8. lift, elevator

P.6

1. connect   2. together   3. surf   4. search, information

P.7

1. B   2. C   3. A